Disney
CLUB PENGUIN
Chillin' with Friends

By Leigh Olsen

Grosset & Dunlap

ISBN 978-0-448-45095-7

10 9 8 7 6 5 4 3 2 1

TOURS
NIGHT CLUB
GIFT SHOP

Chillin' with Friends

Friendship and fun are the best things about Club Penguin. This island of ice and snow is the perfect playground for anything you and your friends can think of, whether you want to play a game, get an awesome job, or throw a party! All you need is your imagination.

Friendly Features

Sometimes it can be tricky getting friends to meet in the same place at the same time. But Club Penguin has some features that can help you out the next time you're planning an activity.

Penguin Standard Time (PST)

Once you and your friends have picked a server and part of the island, use the clock at the Snow Forts to choose a time to meet. This clock is set to Penguin Standard Time. It may be different than your home clock, but Penguin Standard Time is the same all over the world. That helps penguins in different time zones meet up more easily.

Tomorrow

In 10 minutes

Party at my igloo!!!

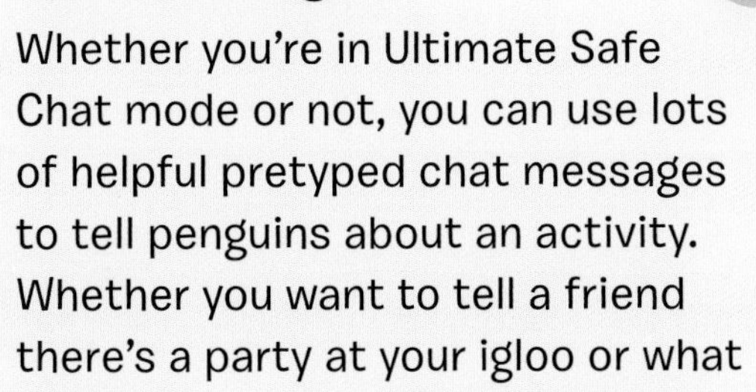

Chat Messages

Whether you're in Ultimate Safe Chat mode or not, you can use lots of helpful pretyped chat messages to tell penguins about an activity. Whether you want to tell a friend there's a party at your igloo or what time an activity is happening, these messages can do the trick.

Postcards

Postcards are a quick way to invite penguins to join you in an activity. There are postcards inviting friends to every part of the island! Postcards are also a great way to make new friends. Open your Penguin Mailbox at the top left of your screen to view, buy, and send postcards.

Pizza Parlor Play

On Club Penguin, work is as much fun as play! There are all kinds of jobs available at the Pizza Parlor. You and your friends can each pick a job and help keep customers happy—and fed!

The Pizza Parlor is one of the most happening spots on the island. And waiting tables there is a blast! Just approach a table of hungry penguins and ask for their order. Then you can bring them a piping hot pizza—or anything else they want!

Tossing dough is easier than it looks. To be a pizza chef, you just need to buy a chef's hat and apron from the Penguin Style catalog. Many chefs double as servers so that they can take their customers' orders and then toss a fresh pizza pie right at their table!

Other awesome Pizza Parlor jobs include being a manager or owner, a cashier, a pizza delivery penguin, or a musician on the Pizza Parlor stage.

Hangin' at the Coffee Shop

Love the relaxed atmosphere at the Coffee Shop? This might be a great place for you to work—or just play!

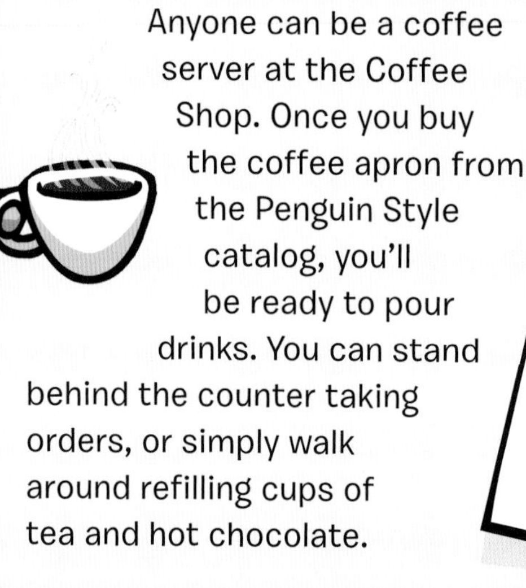

Anyone can be a coffee server at the Coffee Shop. Once you buy the coffee apron from the Penguin Style catalog, you'll be ready to pour drinks. You can stand behind the counter taking orders, or simply walk around refilling cups of tea and hot chocolate.

You can come up with other Coffee Shop jobs, too. Maybe you want to be an owner or a manager, watching over your "employees" and checking to see if your customers are happy. You can be a baker or a janitor, too. Whatever job you can think of, you can do it!

With its calm mood, the Coffee Shop is also a great place to put on a poetry reading. Or you can be a stand-up comedian, entertaining guests with jokes.

Groovin' at the Night Club

If your friends are music and dance fanatics, the Night Club's a great place to hang out! You can give yourself a job there, or just have a good time dancing the day away.

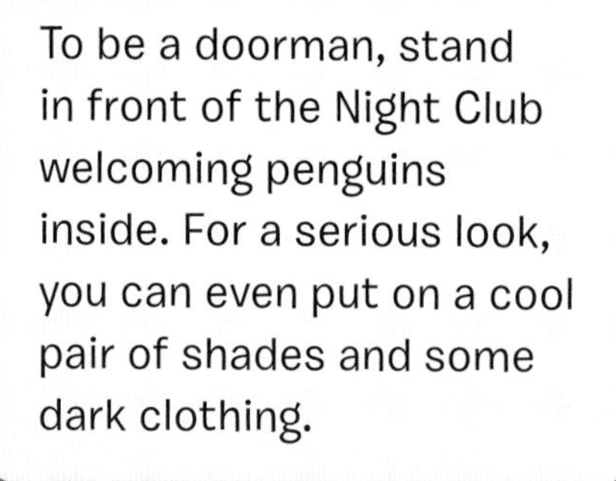

To be a doorman, stand in front of the Night Club welcoming penguins inside. For a serious look, you can even put on a cool pair of shades and some dark clothing.

Want to be where all the action's at? Head indoors and be a DJ, playing some hot dance tunes from behind the turn-table. You can even play DJ3K to earn some coins for your time behind the turntable. Or go around encouraging penguins to boogie on the dance floor!

You and your friends can organize a synchronized dance, where a bunch of penguins move and groove in time with one another. You just have to make sure everyone clicks the dance icon at the exact same time. You can do this anywhere on Club Penguin, but the Night Club is a popular place.

Sports Mania

Club Penguin is a sports-lover's paradise! All you need is some equipment and a place to play.

The Penguin Stadium is the ultimate place for sports action. Mosey on over to find out which sport is on. Ice hockey and soccer are popular sports. To play, gather up enough penguins for two teams. You can buy blue or red uniforms and equipment from the Snow and Sports catalog. The puck or ball is waiting in the stadium!

Need encouragement? Find pals to be cheerleaders. The uniforms are in the Snow and Sports catalog. Then find fans to fill the bleachers. You can even get a friend to referee!

Ice hockey's not the only sport on Club Penguin. Depending on the time of year, you can find gear in the Snow and Sports catalog for all kinds of sports including football, dodgeball, soccer, baseball, and more!

Games can be organized anywhere. Turn your igloo into a sports arena and invite your friends over to play. Or play in areas that don't get too busy, like the Forest or the Iceberg.

Penguins in Plays

The Stage is the place to be for aspiring actors, actresses, and directors on Club Penguin. Get your creative friends together and put on a show. It's actually pretty easy!

Plays at The Stage change every month. But each play at The Stage contains at least four acting parts, and every show needs a director. The director can help choose who plays the parts. If you want, you can hold auditions, and each penguin can take turns trying out for the part he or she wants.

Would you rather be behind the scenes? You can be in charge of special effects, handling the supercool Switchbox 3000 in front of The Stage. Or, you can sell tickets at the box office in front of the theater.

There are always costumes available for purchase in the Costume Trunk. Once you're dressed, just open up the script and click on your lines to recite them.

When you're ready to perform, you and your friends can go around the island, inviting penguins to be audience members at your big premiere.

Get Your Game On

You and your penguin pals can play multiplayer mini-games together. But you don't have to bring a friend with you to play. These games are perfect places for meeting new friends!

Head to the Dojo to play *Card-Jitsu* and battle it out for cool ninja belts. Step on one of the mats to play with a buddy, or play with someone new. If you're the first to collect one of each kind of card—water, fire, and snow—or three of a kind, you win!

If you're looking for a laid-back two-player game, try out *Find Four* in the Lodge Attic or *Mancala* in the Book Room. Both games are great for strategy-minded penguins.

When Rockhopper comes to shore, you can play *Treasure Hunt* on the *Migrator*. Grab a friend, get in the sandbox, and work together to dig for buried treasure!

Head to the Ski Hill for some *Sled Racing* action with your buddies. Up to four penguins can race at a time. First to the bottom of the hill wins extra coins!

Party Penguins!

Parties are an awesome way to get lots of your friends in one place to celebrate! You can have a party for your birthday, a party for a holiday, a theme party, or a party for any reason at all!

Penguins are always throwing awesome igloo parties. You can, too! Just unlock your igloo and make sure to let everyone know about your party. You can keep it small, inviting your closest friends, or if you want it to be a big bash, your friends can help you invite penguins from all over the island.

You can have a party anywhere on Club Penguin. The Iceberg, the Dojo, and the Forest are popular spots since there's plenty of room for you and all your friends.

Penguins often have parties with themes, whether it's a costume party, a sports-themed party, or a pirate-themed party. Getting your friends dressed up is the easiest way to start a themed party. Whatever you're into, you can make it a party theme.

Club Penguin Clubs

Do you love to dance? Play an instrument? Have snowball fights? Play ice hockey? Whatever your favorite activity is, you can start a club with penguins who like to do the same thing!

To find penguins to join your club, just ask around. For example, if you're starting an ice hockey league, go hang out at the Ice Rink. You're sure to find friends who are also into ice hockey, and you can ask them to join your club. Once you've got your members, you can hold meetings and assign officers like a president and vice president.

Start a club based on one of your favorite games on Club Penguin. Get together and play at the same time, whether it's a multiplayer game or not. Compare scores and strategies for scoring higher.

You can even pick a club uniform by combining items from the catalogs. Your group will really stand out when you're wearing the same outfit.

Rock On

So you want to be a rock star. Why not start a band? First, you'll need a musical instrument. Keep an eye out for them—they're available from time to time at parties or in the Penguin Style catalog. Then look around for friends who want to join. Give your band a name and you're ready to go!

You can hold band practice to make sure you've got your act down. For some privacy, meet in someone's igloo. Or you can practice just about anywhere on Club Penguin.

If you want to put on a concert, you should first pick a venue. Check out the stages at the Lighthouse, the Pizza Parlor, and The Stage. Or perform anywhere you like, whether it's at your igloo or your favorite Club Penguin spot.

To promote your show, let penguins know where and when it will be. When you're ready to perform, you can introduce yourselves so everyone knows your band's name. Then, just rock and roll!

Snowball Fight!

It's fun throwing snowballs all by yourself, but having big snowball fights is even better! Just click the snowball icon, take aim, and click to throw! Snowball fights often take place at the Snow Forts. You can form teams and duck behind the barriers to avoid getting hit!

You don't have to stick to the Snow Forts for snowball fights. You can organize one anywhere! Get your group of snowball-throwers together beforehand, or just announce a snowball fight out of the blue—anywhere, anytime!

Penguins on Parade

Parades are a great way for you and your friends to celebrate holidays and other big events. You can start a parade anytime—even if you don't have a reason! Just announce there's going to be one, and lead your friends and other penguins around the island.

Many penguins are concerned about the environment. If you want to help promote a greener planet, you and your friends can all turn green and parade around promoting environmentally friendly activities like reducing, reusing, and recycling.

Working Hard in Hard Hats

Club Penguin is a work in progress. And penguins love to rally together to help make it a better place! When new construction is happening, you'll see a construction site under way. You can help fix up a building, renovate a room, or build something completely brand-new and exciting. Sometimes, you can even help Gary the Gadget Guy build his latest invention!

When there's a construction site, you can sometimes find hard hats and drills for free. Get your friends together to drill and help build Club Penguin's latest addition.

Penguins to the Rescue

Want to help penguins in danger? You should join the Rescue Squad! Rescue Squad members are known for their skill and bravery in dangerous situations. The uniform is available every so often in the catalogs. Once you're dressed and ready to go, you and your friends can keep an eye out on the Ski Hill, where the Rescue Squad got its start. Or you can help get penguins to safety in case there's an earthquake, a flood, or an avalanche on Club Penguin.

Swimming safety is important—and lifeguards are always needed where there are swimming penguins. You can be a lifeguard and watch over swimmers at the Underground Pool or the Cove. The lifeguard shirt and whistle are available now and then in the Penguin Style catalog, though you don't need them to look out for swimmers.

Tours Here!

Think you're really familiar with Club Penguin? Once you're forty-five days old, you can take a test to become a Tour Guide. After you pass your test, put on the Tour Guide hat and go to the Tours booth in the Ski Village. Wait there for new penguins who need a tour. Or just begin a tour, and interested penguins will follow. Chances are, you'll make lots of friends this way.

Using the Safe Chat bubbles as you move from room to room, you can easily show new penguins around the island. If you don't feel like giving a tour, you can also hang out in your favorite part of Club Penguin, answering curi-ous penguins' questions.

Top Secret Fun

Once you are thirty days old, you can apply and take the test to become a secret agent. As a secret agent, your duty is to help keep Club Penguin safe. You also get to go to the Secret Agent Headquarters, where you can get assigned to top secret missions.

You'll meet lots of other secret agents at HQ. This is a great place to find friends! You and your secret agent buddies can patrol Club Penguin together, looking out for signs of trouble. You can even come up with your own missions.

More Stuff to Do with Friends!

Try and tip the Iceberg.

Can it be done? No one's sure, but you can always try! Get as many penguins together as you can. Stand on one side of the Iceberg and dance and drill away and see if you can tip it!

Act like a pirate.

You and your friends can wear eye patches and bandannas and pretend you're part of Rockhopper's crew. Arrrgh!

Have a fashion show.

Set up a runway in your igloo using cool flooring, or strut your stuff anywhere on the island. Dress up in your most fashionable clothes and work it down the catwalk.

Be a reporter for *The Club Penguin Times.*

You and your friends can keep an eye out on what's happening around the island and submit reviews, poems, jokes, artwork, and more to the newspaper.

Waddle On

The good times never end on Club Penguin. And hopefully by now you have lots of ideas for all the amazing things you can do with your friends. You might even have some new ideas of your own! All it takes to come up with new, exciting activities is some creative thinking, a little silliness, and, most importantly, some friends. Whatever you love to do for fun, it's possible on Club Penguin!